OLT

Olt unfolds in the course of three vividly de-
scribed interludes between action in the life of
the title character. It is a precisely structured,
enjoyable and highly original, miniature novel. In
Olt the author has discovered a way of looking at
the world: with detached involvement, with
controlled tension and a critical yet hilarious eye;
with love, wisdom and a brutal honesty.

Kenneth Gangemi was born in 1937 and grew up
in Scarsdale, New York. He took an engineering
degree at Troy, New York, but for the past eight
years has not worked as an engineer. He has lived
in various places, but those cities he has lived in
longest and knows best are San Francisco, Los
Angeles, New York and Mexico City. He is
currently living in California and working on a
full-length novel. *Olt* is his first published work,
and a volume of poetry is in preparation.

SIGNATURE SERIES

OLT

a novel

Kenneth Gangemi

CALDER & BOYARS
LONDON

First published in Great Britain 1969 by
Calder and Boyars Ltd
18 Brewer Street London W 1

SBN 7145 0659 1 Cloth edition
SBN 7145 0660 5 Paper edition

Printed in Great Britain by
The Camelot Press Ltd.,
London & Southampton

I

THE PAIN

Robert Olt felt the pain again when he bent
down to pick up a cracker from the floor. He put
a hand to his belly, wondering what the pain was,
and tossed the cracker into a paper bag marked
'Ducks.' He walked over to his bureau and picked
up a slip of paper:

> Man is the species *sapiens*
> of the genus *Homo*
> of the family *Hominidae*
> of the sub-order *Anthropoidea*
> of the order *Primates*
> of the sub-class *Eutheria*

of the class *Mammalia*
of the sub-phylum *Craniata*
of the phylum *Chordata*
of the sub-kingdom *Metazoa*
of the animal kingdom.

Also on top of his bureau was a clipped advertisement that offered, for one dollar, a list of two
hundred uses for sawdust, newspapers, and tin
cans. There was a book about dinosaurs, a folder
describing giant binoculars, a Japanese camera, a
letter from a friend, a map of the city, a bear's
tooth, and a list of forty-two differences between
sunrises and sunsets.

The bear's tooth reminded him of his trip to
the zoo the day before. He remembered the
alarm at four o'clock in the morning, coffee in
the all-night cafeteria, and the deserted streetcar.
He had presented his Zoological Society card at
the gates and been admitted just as the first rays
of sun were striking the treetops. A white pigeon
had flown up from the shadows and flashed into
the sunlight. Robert Olt remembered the morning
when he had crawled out of a sleeping bag and
watched a magnificent sunrise while standing
naked on the rim of the Grand Canyon.

The veterinarian had hurried by, off to treat
cases of barn itch, big head, lumpy jaw, black

scab, breast blisters, blue bag, scabby nose, and ox warbles. Once Olt had watched him take semen from a bull rhinoceros and inseminate a female. He had watched him operate on a hippopotamus, deliver a baby giraffe, and extract a bear's tooth.

Olt had made friends with some of the keepers, and they permitted him to enter the cages. The flying squirrels had glided down to his shoulders, landing with soft *thumps* on his sweater. He had played with the ocelot cubs, and tossed fish-chunks to the dripping otters.

During the winter he had watched the macaques turned out to play in the snow. He had watched the keepers take buckets of neat's-foot oil and long-handled brushes and oil the elephants. They had told him that one of the performing elephants, in order to avoid punishment for mistakes, secretly practiced her act at night.

Olt had seen a bighorn ram mount a small female, forcing her to her knees. He had walked through the Australian collection and seen the kangaroo, boobook, bandicoot, cockatoo, kookaburra, numbat, nardoo, wallaby, wallaroo, and jackeroo. He had gazed with admiration at the furry, black-and-orange scrotum of the Bengal tiger and had wanted to swap.

Robert Olt stopped thinking about the zoo, put on a jacket, and left his room. He was going to visit a girl who lived nearby. It was a warm day, and after he had walked two blocks he took off his jacket and carried it over his shoulder. He saw the market ahead and decided to buy her some peaches.

A bakery and a flower shop adjoined the market. Olt walked into the bakery and sniffed the warm, sweet odours. When his sense of smell became used to the bakery he walked next door to the flower shop and sniffed the flowers. Inside the market he looked into the eye of a fish and saw the image of a straining fisherman. At the fruit counter he looked at a shiny plum and saw the image of a sweating Mexican fruitpicker.

Olt suddenly felt the pain in his belly again and paid for two pounds of peaches and left the market. He thought about his friend as he walked towards her apartment. She had told him about the time when she was fifteen, with stickers in her socks, and dead leaves on the back of her coat, walking alone out of a wood. He knew about her summer job in the department store, where she had gone to work in the mornings without a bra and had come home at night wearing a new one. He knew about the time she had hitchhiked across the country on three dollars.

Once she had been pregnant and looking for an abortion. She had heard that women with German measles could obtain legal abortions, so she found a sick little boy and tried to catch his German measles. She couldn't catch them, but luckily she met the little boy's doctor, and he consented to help her.

When he arrived at her apartment she had just taken a bath. She was lying on the bed, her robe half-open, playing with her Siamese kitten on her bare belly. She smelled of soap. Olt remembered that for a few months, after she had returned from Europe, she had only shaved her right armpit, keeping the left full of silky brown hair.

She thanked him for the peaches and gave him a list of some old college friends she had recently seen. After every name she had written either *growth* or *degeneration*. The list read:

> *degeneration*
> *degeneration*
> *growth*
> *degeneration*
> *degeneration*
> *growth*

degeneration
degeneration
degeneration
degeneration
degeneration

He told her the joke about the woman who wanted to seduce the Pope. She told him about two nightmares: driving through an endless suburb in a station wagon filled with children and collies; and being tossed, naked and bound, into a white-slaver's van. They talked for a few minutes about the possibilities of a tropical garden, the men in the French resistance, the relative decline of the United States, the inefficiency of learning in a classroom and the handful of people who achieve the good life. They talked for a few minutes more about her plans to spend the summer in Denmark, and then he left.

Twenty minutes later Robert Olt bought a newspaper and walked into a cafeteria. At the counter he overheard an old man insist that the *Titanic,* instead of sinking to the ocean floor, had reached equilibrium at a great depth and was still suspended there, slowly revolving in the gloom. He heard a Negro labourer in muddy workshoes order French fries to take out. Olt paid for a cup of black coffee and walked over to a good table by the window.

Three high school girls were sitting at the next table. One girl was looking through the new year-book, and the crackle of the heavy pages reminded him of the special *smell* of a yearbook. There was a new fad: in front of each girl, purposely displayed, was a packet of birth-control pills. Olt watched the girls gather up their books and leave the cafeteria. He looked at their moving backs and buttocks as they walked away and imagined their breasts and bellies.

He picked up the newspaper and began to read. The United Nations was considering the establishment of an international holiday; it would occur on the vernal equinox, the day when all places on earth have equal day and night. Chemists in the perfume industry had succeeded in synthesizing mate-attracting odours that operated below the conscious olfactory range. The planet Venus would be easily visible at midday with the naked eye.

A naturalist reported that the California condor and the whooping crane were now definitely extinct. A political advertisement attacked public libraries as 'socialized books.' An art gallery was showing a collection of thirty-two

framed and mounted death warrants. Another
gallery was showing a collection of nudes: aged
female derelicts, in calendar-girl poses.

A new one-act play was reviewed. The play was a
conversation among seven characters: an infant, a
schoolboy, a young man, three other men aged
thirty, forty-five, and sixty-five, and a senile old
man of eighty, all with the same fingerprints.

Construction had started on the African super-
highways. A surgeon had been accused of grafting
his wife's navel onto her buttock. The body of a
suicide had been discovered in a cheap hotel: no
identification was found, just a geological time
chart and a map of the stars. A man had been
arrested during High Mass at St. Patrick's Cathe-
dral for urinating on the altar.

An editorial-page poem was about a rehabili-
tated man working with a rebuilt bulldozer in a
reclaimed desert. The Internal Revenue Service
announced that there were 15,000 millionaires in
California. A college fraternity had been suspended because three of its members had shaved
a girl's bush. A man from Skagway, Alaska, had
murdered a man from Mazatlán, Mexico, after an
argument over the duration of twilight.

The Psychiatric Society was to view a documentary film on high school orgies. Police were

looking for a man, dressed as an exhumed corpse, who was hiding in cemeteries and sneaking up on people. A columnist wrote about the New Prostitution. Three wirephotos showed Eskimos on motorcycles, Pygmies on waterskis, and the funeral of Henry Luce. Seventy-five tons of apples had been dumped in the Columbia River.

A filler said that in the last 100,000 years 68 billion humans had been born and had died. African antelopes were being introduced into New Mexico to fill 'unoccupied ecological niches.' The Coast Guard had reported over eighty inhabited sea grottos on the Pacific coast. Russia was building the biggest roller coaster in the world.

The sports section had photographs of skiers. Robert Olt suddenly remembered skiing on a sunny spring afternoon and a girl lying in the snow, her knees bent, thighs still spread, vapour rising from her wet pussy into the cold air. She had tossed tiny snowballs at his steaming cock. They had laughed about chapped nipples, and snow-lobsters, and her bush turning white every winter like a snowshoe rabbit.

He turned to the classified ads and read the 'Help Wanted — Men' section. No men were wanted to rebind books, build fountains, paint streetcars, erect junglegyms, or make rowboats.

Olt folded the newspaper and gazed out the window at the passing people. The sidewalks were crowded. He saw two policemen hustle a man into a paddy wagon and felt uneasy, as though his place was also inside the paddy wagon. He saw an old man with a swollen prostate stagger by with two broken suitcases tied with string. He saw a midget bitten by a Pekingese, a man carrying a sign that said 'Keep the Pope off the Moon,' and a Negro boy with a violin case.

Olt left the cafeteria and started walking towards the park. He passed a school where ninth-grade girls in white gym uniforms were playing volleyball outside. He stopped to watch them for a few minutes, thinking of the hot, crowded locker room afterwards. He remembered the time he and two other schoolboys had looked through a roof window and watched thirty naked girls taking showers.

Near the park a street-corner preacher had attracted a small crowd. Olt stopped to listen.

'Do any of you people,' asked the preacher, 'know the difference between God and Santa Claus?'

Everyone was silent. Then a drunk tittered and said, 'There is no God!' and everyone laughed.

Robert Olt entered the park and paused to

look into a baby carriage. He saw a sleeping baby
lying on top of a woman lying on top of an old
woman lying on top of a half-decayed corpse on top
of a brown skeleton on a tan skeleton on a grey
skeleton on a great number of white skeletons,
gradually crumbling into a column of white dust.

At the first bench he sat down and took off
his shoes and socks. He tucked them under the
bench and walked over the freshly cut grass to
the pond. The summer before he had watched
them drain the pond; they had scooped out all
the trash fish, and then restocked with bass and
bluegills. He sat down on the grass. Two boys
were doing something on the other side, and a
minute later he watched a toy sailboat, loaded
with three hamsters, cross the rippled pond.

Robert Olt smiled and lay back on the warm
grass. He felt the sun on his body and imagined
himself basking naked on a sunny island with
hundreds of seals. He tried to picture the faces of
the drugstore and grocery clerks in all his old
neighbourhoods; wondered if it was possible to
run across a pond that was packed with floating
bodies; remembered his eighth-grade science
teacher demonstrating the thermite reaction;
thought of some things he had *not* learned from
people he had *not* known.

He imagined earth as it appeared from the other side of the Milky Way; hundreds of naked children running and laughing along a sunny beach; River Street on a summer evening after a thundershower; Dostoevski and H. G. Wells discussing the evolution of the teachings of Jesus Christ; a naked girl sitting with spread legs at the edge of the surf; a chipmunk peeking out of the eyehole of his bleached skull.

After a few minutes Olt remembered that he had to go to the library and got up and started walking towards the children's playground. He passed an old woman scattering a black powder over the flowerbeds. When he got to the playground he climbed up on the junglegym and sat on the top bar and watched the children playing on the swings and seesaws. A little girl in the sandbox looked up at him and smiled, and he smiled back.

Olt saw a Greek gardener reading an Athens postcard and remembered an old dream. He had dreamed of finding himself in a laughing group of eight men and eight women, quite young, still in their twenties. They had been wearing old European costumes and speaking languages he did not understand. One of the girls had smiled at him. She had introduced herself as the girlfriend of a

Danish student, and had told him that they were his sixteen great-great-grandparents.

Robert Olt smiled again at the little girl in the sandbox. Then he felt the pain in his belly and decided to go to the library. He climbed down from the junglegym, walked back to the bench, put on his shoes and socks, and left the park.

When he arrived at the library he took out a slip of paper. He had written a list of things to look up:

> *TVA*
> *glaciers*
> *American Bison Society*
> *interrogation techniques*
> *advice on dealing with blind people*
> *egret hunters*
> *Japanese relocation*
> *appendicitis symptoms*

He looked over at the prim librarian. She raised her arm and his eyes instantly went to her shaved armpit. Olt saw that she was the type that had a very hairy body. She undoubtedly used electricity, razors, or chemicals to combat the unfashionable hair, and he imagined her running naked in the wilds, leaping over logs, with her hairy arms, hairy thighs, hairy back, hairy breasts, and hairy belly.

Olt looked up at the names inscribed in marble around the rim of the reading room: HOMER— SOCRATES—PLATO—ARCHIMEDES—DANTE— COPERNICUS—KEPLER—GALILEO—NEWTON. He leafed through volume twenty of the encyclopedia — *Sarsaparilla to Sorcery* — and read the article on *sedition*. He read about the men who opposed the Louisiana Purchase. He read why there wasn't a heavier immigration to the Amazon basin.

Olt found an article entitled 'Disasters of the World.' Six pages of disasters were listed, classified as marine disasters, airplane accidents, conflagrations and explosions, earthquakes and volcanos, and hurricanes, tornados, and typhoons.

He read that the Indians loved to put their cold feet into the ripped-open belly of a freshly killed bison. He read why Theodore Roosevelt never created a Lake Tahoe National Park. He read about the naturalist who walked northward with the spring from the Gulf of Mexico to the Canadian border. He looked up *appendicitis* and quickly decided to go to the clinic after reading the part about reverse peristalsis and faecal vomiting.

Before he left, he stopped in to see the famous mural in the children's library. The mural covered an entire wall: Gulliver, Robin Hood, Ferdinand the Bull, Rumpelstiltskin, Babar, the Headless Horseman, Mowgli, the Jabberwock, the ticking crocodile, Glinda, the Tar Baby, Huckleberry Finn, the Seven Dwarfs, the Roc, Winnie-the-Pooh, Long John Silver, Johnny Appleseed, the Bandersnatch, the Forty Thieves, the Goose Girl, the Blue Ox in the Blue Snow, the Cheshire Cat, trolls, castles, the Enchanted Forest, the Emerald City.

That night, as he lay in his hospital bed, Robert Olt thought about the doctor who was going to remove his appendix the next morning. The doctor's face was dominated by overdeveloped snarling muscles. Every time he spoke the snarling muscles triggered and drew his lips back from his teeth. Olt envied the doctor's hands. They knew the feel of goiters and wrinkled skin, and Olt had always wanted to fondle an old woman's goiter.

Earlier in the evening he had read a pamphlet about a soldier who had been shattered by a land mine at El Alamein and had undergone 410 operations in nine years; and he had sat in a big group of bathrobed people and watched an old Charlie Chaplin film.

Kenneth Gangemi

The lights were turned out in the ward. Robert Olt yawned and moved his legs between the clean hospital sheets. He smiled, thinking of the young nurse who had shaved his belly, and soon fell asleep.

II

THE APPOINTMENT

Robert Olt was lying on his bed listening to music. He looked at his clock and saw that it was twenty after. He had to be there in two hours and forty minutes. It was very important.

He picked up a pad of paper. He had started a list of preferences, and so far he had twenty-one: he preferred plastic to ivory, inhalation to exhalation, Pima cotton to upland cotton, small museums to large museums, the morning rush hour to the evening rush hour, ACLU lawyers to corporation lawyers, nuzzling girls to fondling girls, *Sequoia sempervirens* to *Sequoia gigantea,*

motorcycles to automobiles, the vernal equinox
to the autumnal equinox, Greenland Eskimos to
Alaskan Eskimos, travelling south to travelling
north, two-person conversations to four-person
conversations, Mount *Tacoma* to Mount *Rainier,*
curved lines to straight lines, mammoths to
mastodons, warm days in spring to cool days in
summer, random walks to planned walks, wild
strawberries to farm strawberries, Greek alphabet
soup to Russian alphabet soup, and brown buttocks to white buttocks.

Olt put the list aside and thought about the
day before. During the morning he had gone for
a long walk. He had seen a candy factory with
sourball machines, jellybean machines, candycane
machines, gumdrop machines, and lollypop
machines; a sweatshop of six Negroes making
earmuffs; die-casting machines producing 3000
plastic crucifixes per hour; old men with Einstein
haircuts carving ships' figureheads and cigar-store
Indians and merry-go-round animals.

During the afternoon he had visited the Cocoa
Exchange, watched an ice sculptor, called up a
friend, seen an old western, and bought a silent
dog whistle for the zoo. He had overheard a
number of conversations: two busboys speaking
Tagalog, two cocoa brokers talking shop, two old

men arguing about World War II, two girls talking about clothes, boys, and the curse, and two homosexuals talking about labia flapping in the breeze.

Robert Olt stopped thinking about the day before. He sat up on his bed and looked at the books on his table: Emerson's *Essays*, Thoreau's *Walden*, Whitman's *Leaves of Grass*, Mencken's *American Language*, Hemingway's *For Whom the Bell Tolls*, and Mills' *White Collar*.

Olt put on a jacket and left his room. It was a warm day, and after he had walked two blocks he took off his jacket and carried it over his shoulder. He saw a telephone booth ahead and decided to call his girlfriend.

He thought about her while the number was ringing. She used child-sized dishes to help control her weight. She was going to throw her pink pills out the window on the day she was thirty Her mother had once raised money for the Spanish Civil War by raffling herself off at a party. Her father had covered the war as a news-reel photographer and had later been killed in World War II.

She had told him the joke about the *Reader's Digest*, the joke about what the whale said to the submarine, and the joke about the prostitute with poison ivy. She had told him about her college roommate, still in her tennis outfit, jumping into a taxi and going downtown to turn a $100 trick. She didn't like the way he sniffed under the covers in the morning. She could roll back and kiss her foot. She was clean and neat. She gave good backrubs. She tasted good.

She had lived in England and had told him about the student who had been fined ten pounds for farting at the coronation. She thought it absurd that the Queen appeared on more stamps and coins than men like Shakespeare and Darwin and Churchill. She had told him about her girlfriend in London who went to the funerals of artists and writers in order to meet people. She thought Canadians were even more friendly than Americans.

She was originally from New Zealand and had told him all about the fierce Maoris, a sheep-killing parrot called the kea, the giant moa, her pet kiwi, and the six-hour ferryboat ride to Australia. She had a collection of beautiful colour postcards from all over the world. She liked to walk barefoot along the beach with her two Siamese cats. When she was in New Zealand she loved to work naked in her greenhouse of tropical flowers.

There was no answer. Olt hung up and left the telephone booth. Ten minutes later he bought a newspaper and walked into the cafeteria. At the counter he overheard two men arguing about Nijinsky: whether or not he had ever achieved the *entrechat dix*, crossing and uncrossing the feet ten times in a single leap. He overheard a couple arguing about Marxism and Mexico and remembered a story about a man who had hypnotized his wife: whenever she bugged him, a snap of his fingers would give her an overwhelming desire to take a nap: she got lots of sleep, he got lots of peace.

Robert Olt looked up at the clock. He still had two hours and ten minutes before he had to be there. It was very important. He found a slip of paper in his pocket and read it:

Loudest noise ever heard: 1883, island of Krakatoa. Audible in Australia 2000 miles away. Much louder than any H-bomb blast. Volcanic eruption. Blew off half the island. Final blast had enough sound energy to circle the world seven times. Left records of its passing on all the recording barometers in the world.

He put it back in his pocket, paid for a cup of

black coffee, and walked over to the good table
by the window. It was his favourite table. It was
on his list of the twenty-two best places in the
city. He liked to watch the people passing by.

Olt stirred his coffee and thought about some
other things he liked to do. He liked sitting on
the stone rims of fountains and dipping his arm
into the cool water; thinking of his grandmother
as a pink-cheeked sixteen-year-old girl; seeing the
flash of rufous when a red-tailed hawk banked;
watching the rain change the colours of the city;
reading in bed next to his sleeping girlfriend.

He liked sitting on good stoops, letting babies
grasp his finger, leaning over fences to pick black-
berries, watching college girls playing tennis,
looking down into brooks, smelling steaks on
charcoal grills, watching children entering a
circus, making the first footprints on a snow-
covered wharf.

Robert Olt picked up the newspaper and began
to read. The United Nations was exhibiting a
work of sculpture made of half-melted and fused
coins; the coins had been given by children from
all over the world. Police had discovered the
bodies of two more derelicts killed by injections
of poison. The Parks Department was planting
small ornamental trees that would provide a

continuous sequence of bloom throughout the spring and summer. Ten students had been arrested at City Hall for releasing hundreds of rats trapped alive in tenements.

Doctors had successfully transplanted a dead man's scalp to a bald man and were setting up a scalp bank. The graduating class at Harvard included seventeen students of Puerto Rican descent. Humboldt penguins were being introduced along the California coast. The archbishop had granted permission for priests and nuns to attend drive-in movies.

A political advertisement attacked air polution control as being 'communist-inspired.' An advertisement by a conservation group urged people not to buy leopard-fur coats or polar-bear rugs. A filler said that Australia is over twice the size of India but supports only one-fortieth of India's population. Another filler said that Alexander was twenty-six when the priests proclaimed him the Living God.

A wirephoto showed a woman's legs sticking out of rubble. A professor at the University of California had criticized the absurd subjects of many Ph.D. dissertations. An art gallery was exhibiting a series of black-and-white photographs entitled *Afternoon of an Iceberg*. A manufacturer of power tools had presented a well-known sculptor with a $50,000 'dream studio'.

Mexico had designated an enormous area of tropical rainforest as a national wildlife refuge. A medical student had been convicted of performing an abortion on his mother. A letter to the editor accused the book reviewers of being 'arid, academic, and anglomaniac.' Another letter proposed that Potter's Field be replaced by weekly mass cremations.

Cuba had announced an international competition for the design of a tropical zoo. An astronomer had estimated that life existed on fifty million planets in the galaxy. Vermont and California had agreed to exchange 10,000 sugar maple seedlings for 10,000 redwood seedlings. Two girls had told police how they had been taken to a wild party and forced to dance and strip on a table.

Death Valley had recorded a temperature of 134°. An airline had awarded round-trip tickets for South America to twenty young artists. A climatologist had stated that the increase in atmospheric carbon dioxide was already changing the world's climate. The American Nazi Party was sponsoring an exhibition of German combat art.

Olt read about a Soviet-US bridge across the

Bering Strait, Christmas parties at the Missing Persons Bureau, the rise of college-educated call girls, arctic storage for farm surpluses, *The Manhattan Express,* a Nobel prize for film, skunks in the subway, the Dollar Theatre, diverting the Gulf Stream, a museum of architecture, the arrest of a midget prostitute, the Art Students Ball, colour photomurals of the United States, a flower show on an old ferryboat, diamonds smuggled in tampaxes, the Church of Nevada, full moon parties, miniature kangaroos as pets, and *The Handbook of Rape.*

He read about electric bubble-taxis, Japanese bullfights, skyscraper universities, California supermarkets, anti-VD vaccines, porpoise races, cardboard coffins, 100-pound turkeys, Chinese cowboys, skin-diving safaris, Hitler dolls, power toboggans, poker schools, butterfly farmers, Shanghai subways, chicken bricks, Henry Luce, motorcycle raffles, midget surgeons, plastic manacles, nude ballet, Australian gamblers, paperback reform, Masai milkshakes, bearded clams, solar crematories, dwarf Arabs, and chocolate dinosaurs.

He turned to the classified ads and read the 'Help Wanted — Men' section. No men were wanted to repair greenhouses, dam brooks, build sailplanes, paint tugboats, or make surfboards.

Robert Olt folded the newspaper, looked up at the clock, and gazed out the window at the passing people. The sidewalks were crowded. He saw a young man with three children and imagined a salmon with three lampreys. He saw a portable radio and imagined the little hands of all the Japanese girls that made it. He saw a woman from India and imagined a ruby rolling off a fiery skull.

At the museum he had imagined his fossilized skeleton on display, crushed and broken, half the jaw missing, supported by plaster and wire. He had looked at a grove of trees and seen clipper ships. He had looked at a map and seen the autumn colours beginning in Maine and slowly spreading southward. He had held an ice-cube up to the sun and seen snow-capped Mount Shasta, the Sacramento River, and San Francisco Bay. He had looked at the sunrise and seen a wave of opening flowers spreading across the continent.

After a few minutes Olt took a pencil stub from his pocket and began to doodle on the paper napkin:

> *Robert Olt Born!. . .Olt City. . .Oscar Olt*
> *. . .Doctor Olt. . .Otto Olt. . .the office Olt*
> *. . .Olt Ocean. . .the planet Olt. . .Octopus*
> *Olt. . .Olt University. . .Ohio Olt. . .oil of*

Olt. . .Bobby Olt. . .Olt and otter. . .Hotel
Olt. . .the Oltmobile. . .Olt Incorporated. . .
Officer Olt. . .old Olt. . .Oath of Olt. . .
Oklahoma Olt. . .Olt the troll. . .Olt Island
. . .Omsk Olt. . .Oltology. . .Olt in Orbit!. . .
Pope Olt. . .Olt Industries. . .President Olt
. . .Olt Park. . .Citizen Olt. . .old man Olt
. . .Oltocracy. . .Oooooolt. . .Olt Street. . .
Robert Olt Dead!

He left the napkin on the table, walked out of the cafeteria, and headed towards the bookstore. He saw two students crossing the street and remembered his trips to the universities. Every autumn for the past three years he had spent a week at a different university. He enjoyed a week at a university the way people enjoyed a week at a resort. He *delighted* in the facilities of a good university. He liked the trimmed lawns, the pretty girls, the well-kept tennis courts, the peaceful shaded campuses, the vaulted reading rooms of the great libraries, the excitement of the cool October mornings, the bustling university streets with students, cafes, and bookstores.

Two blocks from the cafeteria he spotted a prostitute. He turned around and shadowed her for a few minutes. She reminded him of the illustrated *History of Prostitution* he had just finished. He remembered reading about the golden age of temple prostitutes, ten-cent prostitutes in ancient Athens, waterfront prostitutes and cemetery prostitutes, the patron saint of prostitutes, cathedrals financed by the prostitute-tax, prostitutes and the Popes, medieval processions of naked prostitutes, the carnival of the prostitutes, brothels with phallus-shaped signs, medieval orders of prostitute-nuns, floating brothels in China, brother-and-sister teams from Macao, identical twins as prostitutes, Nazi brothels with military organizations, *The Prostitute's Handbook,* the waitress-prostitute-charwoman sequence, college girls as prostitutes, prostitutes dressed as cheerleaders, prostitutes in Girl Scout uniforms.

Robert Olt shadowed the prostitute until she entered a bar. Then he turned around and continued walking towards the bookstore. Every few minutes he backed up against the stores and paused to look at pedestrians, clouds, and the tops of buildings. He looked at a soaring seagull as though it was rare as an eagle; saw the seagull evolve backwards into a pterodactyl and soar right through a building; looked through the wall of the building and saw a young girl contemplating her tampax string, a skinny black boy on a fat white woman, and a man reading *Journal of a Lesbian Slave-Trader.*

Olt passed a movie theatre and smelled the warm odour of popcorn and red carpets. The girl selling tickets told him it was ten after. He had almost an hour. There was still time for the bookstore.

He decided to take a short cut and turned into an alley. It was very dark. He stepped on the leg of a derelict and felt the flesh roll over the bone. He immediately had a vision of — *crack, snap* — stepping through the rib cage of a dead and rotten baby. He saw himself hopping away on one foot, trying to shake it off.

Olt left the alley and continued walking towards the bookstore. He looked in a bakery window at a display called 'Cookies of the World.' He stopped in to see the German combat art. He looked in the window of a pet shop and remembered reading about the game a naturalist used to play with his pet coati-mundi: the man would try to touch the little snout before it was tucked under the coati-mundi's arm.

Olt crossed the street to avoid a mentally-disturbed man who was shouting at pedestrians. He looked in the window of a novelty store and saw a Japanese urinal-toy: a tiny turbogenerator that would light a tiny bulb. He looked in the window of a motorcycle dealer and saw a model

called 'The Walt Whitman.' He saw a message
written on a wall:

> *Put the Clowns into the Senate!*
> *Put the Senators into the Circus!*

Near the bookstore a travel agency displayed a
Robinson Crusoe Kit that contained all the
essentials for a tropical island. There was also a
display of tropical fruits: mangos, papayas,
sapodillas, cherimoyas, pitayas, granadillas,
zapotes, and *guanábanas.* There was a colour
photograph of a beautiful English girl reading the
South China Morning Post.

The displays reminded him of his plans for a
one-year Pacific trip. He planned to travel from
San Francisco to Hawaii, from Hawaii to Tahiti,
from Tahiti to New Zealand, from New Zealand
to Australia, from Australia to Singapore, from
Singapore to Hong Kong, from Hong Kong to
Japan, and from Japan back to San Francisco.

He had other trips planned for Asia, Africa,
and South America. He had never watched
coastal rains from a tropical mountain, ridden the
ferry between India and Ceylon, sunned on Black
Sea beaches, seen Mars at dawn over Tahiti, trav-
elled through Central Asia, crossed the Burma-
Tibet frontier, ridden horses in the Caucasus,

gone swimming on the Turkish Riviera, climbed the Ruwenzori Mountains, sailed in the Celebes Sea, walked about Rio at dawn, ridden the Cape-to-Cairo railroad, or drifted down the Amazon at night.

He had never seen the fishes of the coral reef, volcanos erupting at night, parades of Chinese children, kangaroos splashing through the surf, forests of Spanish mahogany, typhoons in the China Sea, lava advancing in a jungle, tigers swimming from Java to Bali, the colours of a Chinese harbour, or the constellations of the southern sky.

Once he had daydreamed about settling on a South Sea island of green marble and royal palms and white sand, a bearded old man watching his twenty-two wives and fifty-seven children bathing naked in the surf.

Robert Olt entered the bookstore and looked through a new edition of *Hamlet.* It was essentially a comic-book format, but with excellent pen-and-ink drawings, and was very expensive. He looked at a book of colour photographs entitled *Sunsets in the Painted Desert.* He looked at some cartoons from India that showed Gandhi at the movies, Gandhi on a motorcycle, Gandhi in sneakers, Gandhi playing golf, Gandhi on waterskis, Gandhi in Tiffany's, and Gandhi lifting weights.

Olt saw a book about Brazil and remembered the time he had been introduced to a man at a party. They had talked together for a long time, and he had liked him more and more. He had been very interested in the Amazon at the time, and he had asked the man if he had ever read anything on the subject. 'Have I read about the Amazon?' the man had said. 'Why, I've read everything on the Amazon that I can get my hands on!'

Olt looked through a book on the sexual behaviour of American women and found a graph entitled 'Prostitute Population.' On one axis was *per cent of females between 18 and 45,* and on the other axis was *dollars.* He saw *The Brothers Karamazov* and remembered searching through it when he was a boy and finding the formula for gunpowder:

> . . . *twenty-four parts of saltpeter, ten of sulfur, and six of birchwood charcoal. It's all pounded together, mixed into a paste with water, and rubbed through a tammy sieve . . . .*

In a book on mortuary science he read a chapter entitled 'The Dynamics of Decomposition.' It contained a series of colour photographs showing the process of decomposition of a corpse. He looked through a book of motion-picture stills: *The Maltese Falcon, Modern Times, The Bridge on the River Kwai, Pather Panchali, A Streetcar Named Desire, The Bicycle Thief, Paths of Glory, The Seventh Seal, The Treasure of the Sierra Madre, Citizen Kane.*

Robert Olt looked through the journal of a nineteenth-century Englishman who lived in the days when sweatshops were often private brothels for the owners. The man was delighted with his young employees, made different by their work. Olt read about factory girls on rubbish heaps, laundry girls with steaming bodies, bobbin girls on cotton bales, cider girls in apple bins, stable girls on carriage blankets, and bakery girls with powdered arms.

He suddenly realized that he had completely forgotten about the time and replaced the book and walked outside. It was much too late to go. He started walking up the street. After a few minutes he decided to return to his room and lie on the bed and listen to music.

III

THE FORECAST

Robert Olt was sitting at his desk looking through his dictionary. He discovered that the word he wanted was not there and that he would have to look it up in the unabridged dictionary in the library. He took a pencil and added the word to his list of words not in the dictionary. When the list became a little longer he was going to send a copy to the editors of the dictionary. He read over the list:

auctorial *logophile*
achphenomenon *sabra*
polymath *cacotopia*

chemoreception	*privatism*
parabiotic	*meshuggah*
android	*theophagy*
superogation	*slushpile*
supernova	*schlack*
flack	*neophilia*
paramnesia	*souk*
kitsch	*quokka*
lumpen	*virologist*
oneiric	*zook*
frottage	*yonic*

Olt put the list aside and leaned back in his chair and thought about the day before. During the morning he had walked down by the waterfront. He had seen the cat from the freighter *China Bear* mate with the cat from the freighter *African Dawn*. He had watched the outfitting of a scientific vessel that was to sail up the Orinoco River and collect tropical vertebrates. He had seen Animal Shelter employees lower a cage of stray dogs into the water. He had watched workmen casting play sculpture in a waterfront park, boys flying a radio-controlled jet seaplane, and ragged old women fishing with droplines. The waterfront activity had reminded him of the time he had gone island-hopping with a motorcycle in the Caribbean.

After the twelve o'clock whistle he had bought a roast beef sandwich and a can of cold beer and climbed up on some sacks of coffee beans to have lunch. He had thought of the millions of other people in the time zone who were also sitting down and eating lunch. He had thought of the thousands of white-collar workers who were fighting for stools at crowded lunch counters.

Olt remembered watching a gang of longshoremen sit down and open up lunchboxes and begin to eat. The longshoremen had laughed and joked, and they almost threw one man into the water. When someone told them it was time to get back to work, they laughed and lit up cigarettes and told him to go fuck himself.

After lunch Olt had walked away from the waterfront and boarded a bus and ridden up to the museum. On a warm summer day, on a busy street, there was nothing like looking out the open window of a slow-moving bus for a series of small and pleasant stimulus changes. Olt remembered the women who had filled up the bus. Most of them had been wearing sleeveless dresses, and he remembered looking up from his seat at their exposed armpits. He had examined their armpits closely. He had always felt a vague interest and a curious attraction in the armpits of women.

At the museum he had seen a free wildlife film entitled *Wyoming Spring* that showed the unfolding of flowers, butterflies emerging from cocoons, rainbow trout spawning, eagles building a nest, and the birth of a fawn. In the past he had seen a film about the world's most beautiful islands, a film about the life of a jaguar cub in the Mexican jungle, and a film about the Roraima plateau, the basis of Conan Doyle's *The Lost World*.

After the film he had walked down the dark hallway that was lined with jars of foetal monsters. He had looked at the enormous murals that showed herds of imperial bison on the prairies, mammoths along the Ohio River, and saber-toothed tigers in California. He had presented his museum membership card and been permitted to enter the workshops, where he had watched entomologists loading water cartridges in twelve-gauge shells for tropical butterflies, paleontologists separating saber-tooth skulls from asphalt, herpetologists assembling a python skeleton, and mammalogists skinning a baby giraffe.

Robert Olt stopped thinking about the museum. He sat up in his chair and looked at the things on his desk: Indian head pennies, fishing bobbers, cocoons in jars, *Ulysses*, clippings from

London, a ski-patrol pack, *Stedman's Medical Dictionary,* passport photos, an appendix preserved in plastic, topographic hiking maps, Peterson's *Field Guide to the Birds.* He read over his list of things-to-do:

> *science films*
> *mail book to Lydia*
> *see Willet*
> *Russian posters*
> *tiger cubs*
> *Bunsen burner*
> *clambake*

Olt walked over to his bookcase and looked through some of his favourite books. In Montaigne's *Essays* he read about the old French landowner who on cold winter nights made two peasant girls sleep in his bed. In Forster's *Two Cheers for Democracy* he read the essay 'What I Believe.' In *The Voyage of the Beagle* he read how Darwin responded to the sight of a naked man on a horse. In *Paul Bunyan* he read about the lumberjack who was so fast he could blow out the bunkhouse lamp and get in his bunk before it was dark.

Olt suddenly became aware of the sounds of a parade. He walked over to his open window and

saw people gathered on the next corner. He
quickly left his room and hurried downstairs and
joined them.

It was a small military parade. He read the name
tags as the soldiers marched by: SMITH—
JOHNSON—WILLIAMS—JONES—BROWN—
MILLER—DAVIS—ANDERSON—WILSON—
THOMPSON. Olt remembered the part in
Dostoevski about the soldiers tossing babies into
the air and catching them on bayonets. He remembered reading about the war in China. Sixteen-
year-old girls had their feet sliced, gravel put into
the wound, and the wound sewn up, and then were
raped by forty or fifty soldiers every day.

After the parade had passed Olt started
walking down the street. Ten minutes later he
bought a newspaper and entered the cafeteria. At
the counter he stood near two nuns in order to
overhear their conversation. He paid for a cup of
black coffee and walked over to the good table
by the window.

Three old women were sitting at the next
table. They were eating pastries and talking about
other old women who were in hospitals. He
remembered that on Christmas Day the cafeteria
was full of dressed-up old men who sat alone and
ate the Special Turkey Dinner.

Robert Olt stirred his coffee and looked up at the enormous relief map of the United States that covered one wall of the cafeteria. It was a beautiful map. He looked at his favourite parts of the country. He especially liked the southern Atlantic coast, Florida, the Florida Keys, southern Louisiana, the Southwest, and the mountain states: Nevada, Montana, Utah, Idaho, Wyoming, Colorado.

Olt looked at the map and remembered walking on a deserted beach in Florida and turning around and looking back at his footprints in the sand; walking about Boston during a quiet snowfall; watching the United Nations employees arriving at work on a summer morning; hitchhiking from Chicago to Los Angeles along Route 66; swimming in a sparkling lake in a desert canyon in Nevada; riding the ferry across the Mississippi River to New Orleans; seeing the sun sink into the Pacific from a cliff in California.

He remembered watching the cantaloupe harvest in the Imperial Valley; listening to distant jazz on a summer night in Kansas City; resting in the shade of ruins in New Mexico; seeing the eighteen canyons of the Colorado River; spotting a peregrine in the Sierras; watching thunderclouds build up over the Gulf coast; seeing the green

flash in the Arizona desert; sitting on the library
steps in San Francisco; riding horses in the
Tetons; watching rush-hour streams of people in
Manhattan; sitting quietly in a redwood forest in
California.

Robert Olt picked up the newspaper and began
to read. Japan was building mineral-extracting
ships that propelled themselves through the sea
by ejecting the water they had processed. A gas
explosion had blown off sixteen manhole covers.
The Pope had warned against 'the virus of
rationalism.' A breed of chickens had been developed that laid nothing but double-yolked eggs.

The Marine Corps had hired a team of psychia-
trists to find out why so many ex-marines went
berserk. A physician had stated that one-third of
the infant mortality rate was due to 'irreducible
birth and genetic accident.' An avant-garde order
of nuns had adopted a habit similar to the outfits
of airline stewardesses. A filler said that Joe Hill
died in front of a Utah firing squad in 1915.

The Sunday topic at the Unitarian Church was
to be The New Materialism. A scientist had pre-
dicted that in fifty years an optimum ocean level
would be fixed and maintained by an International Icecap Control Commission. A brokerage
firm had published a booklet entitled *A Guide to*

Humanitarian Investments. A theatre was running a two-week festival of science-fiction and horror movies.

Five African countries were planning to pool their resources and manufacture an automobile called the *Simba.* A columnist wrote of a man who had thin slices from his amputated arm encased in plastic and used as coasters. A filler said that in the USSR a full professor is paid twice as much as a factory manager. Another filler said that there were 200 million girls between the ages of sixteen and twenty-one.

The International School of City Planning had established a minimum admission age of thirty. A new book of poetry was dedicated to the unidentified poets who had perished in German crematoriums. An anthropologist had called the racial mixture of the modern Hawaiian a preview of ultimate world man. A foundation was sponsoring an architectural competition for a house of prostitution. An airline was advertising a Sunset Flight: it took off from New York at sunset and landed in Los Angeles at sunset.

Russian scientists had discovered a large number of frozen Pleistocene animals. A new novel was about the anxieties of an overweight woman in Caracas. A sculptor had claimed that the highest art was the sculpture of vertebrate forms in non-deteriorating material. A drug company had developed a quick-acting pill that stimulated secretion from the Bartholin glands. The Parks Department had purchased fifty purple martin houses built by the handicapped.

Seventeen countries were to exhibit automatic doughnut-making machines. A psychologist had stated that the suicidal student has a desire to destroy himself because he can no longer tolerate the discrepancy between how he appears to himself and how he would like to be. Two professors were to debate the compatibility of existentialism and Marxism. A sociologist had produced an LP record made from taped conversations in a Lesbian bar.

Olt read about high school seniors taking out ninth-grade girls, revolutionists opening crates of submachine guns, a swallow's nest on a ferryboat, the Committee for Communication with China, a naked man in a tree, tame deer for the parks, Hawaiian skating rinks, waitresses drifting into prostitution, *Onkel Toms Hütte,* tea dances at the Teamsters Union, the coming Ice Age, the Church of the Four-Leaf Clover, a film called *Coca-Cola Douche,* an invasion of snowy owls, Mark Twain pennies, muddy shoes in the White House, the

world's largest cafeteria, baby porpoises at the
aquarium, girl gymnasts in bikinis, and *California
Arts* magazine.

He read about the Condor Legion, white-collar
crime, Arizona roadhouses, antique plastic,
bayonet designers, riverboat poker, chicken-fried
steaks, Andes tunnels, runaway girls, billboard
burners, Detroit Jews, nudist nuns, time capsules,
roof tennis, Mexican *machismo,* plastic tomb-
stones, French pilots, graffiti hunters, computer
thieves, robot prostitutes, sea otters, *kif* pipes,
Sex Police, owl farms, and Ford goons.

Olt turned to the weather forecast. The next
day was to be sunny and warm, with temperatures in the nineties. He turned to the classified
ads and read the 'Help Wanted — Men' section.
No men were wanted to build terrariums, repair
sailboats, tag salmon, paint cottages, or make
salads.

Robert Olt folded the newspaper and gazed
out the window at the passing people. The sidewalks were crowded. The cafeteria was located at
one of those intersections where many different
kinds of people crossed paths. He watched the
people for a few minutes and then finished his
coffee and left the cafeteria.

Olt started walking toward the department

store. He passed a garbage-can alley, saw a pile of black-and-white rubbish, and for an instant thought it was a dead nun. He saw an interracial couple with a child and automatically compared the skin colour of the child with the skin colours of the parents. He saw a pregnant woman and a fat man look at each other as they passed. He saw two old women stagger into a health food store.

Olt saw a man spit and remembered reading that dried sputum might contain virulent TB germs for eight months. He saw a woman alcoholic with the fixed eyes, swollen legs, and unsteady walk that meant Wernicke's syndrome. He saw a shaking old Negro having difficulty stepping up on the curb and wondered if he had tertiary syphilis. Olt remembered the scrawled message he had seen on a prophylactic vending machine in New Orleans:

> *dont buy this gum*
> *it taste like rubber*

Outside a movie theatre he looked at the stills of a documentary about the R.A.F. fighter pilots during the Battle of Britain. In the window of a jewellery store he looked at a display of Chinese mortuary jade, used to close up the nine orifices of the body after death. In the window of *Le Snack-Bar* he watched the black hands of the African cook make yellow French omeletts.

Robert Olt walked into the department store and went directly to the TV department, where he sniffed the ozone and watched a programme that showed high school kids dancing. In the jewellery department he stood in a crowd of people and watched a silversmith demonstrate the lost-wax process. In the pet department he looked at a cage of saw-whet owls and a cage of baby coati-mundis. In the record department he picked up a free Köchel listing and then sat in a soundproof cubicle and listened to a new comedian. In the gourmet department he tasted a free sample of smoked sturgeon.

Once he had sat in on the orientation movie shown to new salesgirls. Once he had spent two hours riding up and down the escalators on the last Saturday before Christmas. That was the Christmas they had fired Santa Claus when a newspaper disclosed that he had been a communist.

In the book department Olt looked through *The Ideal University*, *The Future of the Protestants Ethic*, and *The Psychology of Political Affiliation*. He read a story about a man who equipped a soundproof room and took pairs of girls there and subjugated them. He looked at a beautiful book of colour photographs entitled *Tropical Ports.*

Olt looked through *Tricks of the Trade,* written by an ex-prostitute. He read through a collection of suicide notes. He looked at *How to Pass as Upper Class.* He looked in a book for children:

> ....*The Arabs told the Eskimos what to do during sandstorms. The Eskimos told the Arabs what to do during blizzards. The Arabs told the Eskimos about camels, tents, goats, and dates. The Eskimos told the Arabs about walruses, kayaks, igloos, and blubber....*

Olt walked through the department store. He overheard two salesgirls talking about a customer. He watched the manager chase some kids playing department-store tag. He explored the basement and found the kennels where they kept the six Doberman pinschers that patrolled the store at night. He opened a panel and saw what the inside of the escalator looked like. He rode the escalators to the top floor, opened a door that said *For Employees Only,* and stepped out on the roof.

Robert Olt walked to the edge of the roof and

looked down at the people in the street. He remembered the time he and two other school-boys had looked through a roof window and watched thirty naked girls taking showers. He knew he would never do that again.

Olt knew he would never see a meteor striking an iceberg, a bat falling into snow, or a clown on a nun. He knew he would never go to a party and talk to thunderstorm experts, roller-coaster experts, vampire experts, sailplane experts, dinosaur experts, or volcano experts. He knew he would never design bear grottos, furnish a time capsule, live in an orange grove, wade in a vat of mercury, work in the Dead Letter Office, find narwhale tusks on a beach, see a tampax string at the ballet, smell a burning spice warehouse, over-hear two call girls talking shop, or attend a meeting of the Junior League.

Olt knew he would never find a purse con-taining birth-control pills, sketching pencils, and *Les Fleurs du Mal;* see a slow-motion film of bullets striking a condemned man's chest and face; look through an illustrated 1898 brothel-supplier's catalogue; ride on top of a narrow-gauge banana train winding slowly through the jungle; make a training film for prostitutes; see a corpse crushed in a giant hydraulic press; hear

Mozart's *Symphony No. 42* or read *Orwell in Mexico;* see impoverished citizens getting free passes to government brothels; sit on an Alaskan riverbank and eat salmon with eagles and bears; see the woman with the biggest bush in the world; read the *Mars Daily News* while sitting on the trimmed lawn of the University of Venus; see hundreds of naked pregnant women floating on their backs in Great Salt Lake.

Robert Olt left the roof and rode the escalators down and walked out of the department store. He started walking over to a friend's apartment to listen to a new record. After a few minutes he changed his mind and turned around and decided to watch the girls streaming out of high school. Then he changed his mind again and turned around and walked into a magazine store.

In the *New Statesman* he read an article on the secret experiments conducted in the scientific underground in order to evade social pressures and legal barriers. In the *Nation* he read an article entitled 'Vision of an American Sub-Culture.' In the *New Yorker* he saw a good cartoon for his cartoon collection. In *Scientific American* he read about the four hours between somatic death and cellular death.

Olt flipped through *Town and Country* and

titillated his Scott Fitzgerald component. He
looked at *Safari,* a slick African magazine. He
picked up *Cremation* magazine and read a de-
scription of what happens in the retort. He
flipped through *Kill* magazine, *Australian Youth,*
Buffalo Business, Turkey World, and *Muscle Girls.*

Olt picked up a European fashion magazine
and remembered the Canadian girl he had met in
Europe. She had been wearing an Austrian
sweater, Italian blouse, English skirt, French bra,
and American panties. He flipped through the
magazine and thought about his year in Europe.

Inside his suitcase he had carried a card with
his name and address on one side and a quotation
from Rilke on the other:

> *And one has nothing and nobody*
> *and one travels about the world*
> *with a trunk and a case of books*

He remembered sitting at a sidewalk cafe in
Athens and calculating that the columns of the
Parthenon would meet if extended one mile into
the air; being in a wild Greek movie-house during
a slapstick American comedy; wandering into
strange quarters on warm summer nights; sitting
on cotton bales and watching the bustling activity
on the Piraeus wharves; seeing a sixty-year-old

fisherman, lean and tanned, doing pushups from a handstand position; watching a parade of sixteen-year-old schoolgirls in white dresses.

He remembered Paris and the girl with the grass-stained skirt, burying his face in her warm good-smelling breasts, pressing his lips and nose against her warm good-smelling skin; London and the delightful accent of the coloured girl from Jamaica, nude except for her black glasses and woolly bush; Copenhagen and the student who smelled of caramel, was barefoot, and had Alice-in-Wonderland hair; Barcelona and the Spanish prostitute with the glow-in-the-dark crucifix; Vienna and the waitress with red armpit-hair, freckled skin, and beer-garden arms.

Olt thought of the Danish girl who told him that Denmark was *first* on the list of Nobel-prizes-per-one-million-population, and that the United States was *seventh;* the German girl who told him about the Dresden bombing; the English journalist who told him how thrilled she had been upon hearing *Hail to the Chief* and then seeing Kennedy; the American girl who said she viewed her own parents as objectively as she viewed two white rats in a cage; the Swedish girl with the collection of colourful socialist publications; the Dutch girl who told him that Galileo died in the year Newton was born; the Swiss girl who scribbled down a hotel in London, a restaurant in Paris, a sidewalk cafe in Rome; the Norwegian girl who observed that the speed of drinking at sidewalk cafes varies inversely as the price of the drinks; the Italian actress who told him about sixty-year-old men slipping it into sixteen-year-old girls; the Austrian girl who had flown open-cockpit sailplanes in the Alps; the French girl who loved westerns and wanted to visit Tombstone, Cheyenne, Abilene, Laramie, and Laredo.

Robert Olt stopped thinking about Europe and left the magazine store and started walking up the street. He spotted a pretty girl looking in the window of an art gallery and walked over and stood next to her. She was looking at a model of an invention by Alexander Graham Bell. It was a machine for condensing fog with a bellows actuated by the rise and fall of the waves. He talked to the girl for two minutes and learned that she was a Catholic girl in conflict, a small-town girl getting nowhere in the city, and an unmarried girl approaching thirty.

Inside the gallery Olt looked at stark paintings of office scenes and white-collar life; a portrait of a pink young girl who had been dead for a hundred years; a painting of the horror below decks when a slave ship was scuttled; an enormous sculpture entitled *Cunt;* a diagram of the planet earth showing the optimum angle of inclination, the optimum time of rotation, and the optimum path of orbit; a painting entitled *Old Actress Listening to Recorded Applause from a Past Performance;* slick paintings of science-fiction scenes; a photograph of the Dada lecture given by thirty-eight lecturers at once; a painting of an ancient procession of priestesses squatting on a golden phallus; a display of new gyroscopes spinning among old, broken gyroscopes; a drawing of a Nazi soldier urinating on a smashed violin.

He looked at a painting of the skeletons of American presidents on exhibit in a Chinese museum; a painting entitled *Naked Schoolgirls Bathing in a Stream;* a series of photographs showing the transformation of a five-year-old girl into a fifty-year-old derelict; a framed blueprint of the Auschwitz raping harness; a reproduction of Rembrandt's *Man Seated Reading at a Table in a Lofty Room;* an aerial photograph of Coney Island on the 4th of July; a painting of Attila choosing from the virgins of a captured village; a model of a one-family tropical island, with mountain, orchard, farm, beach, and lagoon.

Robert Olt left the gallery and started walking up the street. He looked at the people walking towards him. The sidewalks were crowded with white-collar workers hurrying home from work. Olt touched the Köchel listing in his pocket. He remembered the weather forecast and thought of the beach. The next day was to be sunny and warm, with temperatures in the nineties. It would be a good day to go swimming in the ocean.

SIGNATURE is a new series of shorter works, distinguished by the highly personal and imaginative approach of the author to his subject. It will comprise works of poetry and prose, fiction and non-fiction, and will include English and American as well as authors of other nationalities in translation. The volumes are numbered and will be published simultaneously in hardcover and paperback and will often employ typographical innovations which are appropriate to the texts.